# The Whipping Words

PRAISE FOR *STORYSHARES*

"One of the brightest innovators and game-changers in the education industry."
– Forbes

"Your success in applying research-validated practices to promote literacy serves as a valuable model for other organizations seeking to create evidence-based literacy programs."

- Library of Congress

"We need powerful social and educational innovation, and Storyshares is breaking new ground. The organization addresses critical problems facing our students and teachers. I am excited about the strategies it brings to the collective work of making sure every student has an equal chance in life."
– Teach For America

"Around the world, this is one of the up-and-coming trailblazers changing the landscape of literacy and education."
- International Literacy Association

"It's the perfect idea. There's really nothing like this. I mean wow, this will be a wonderful experience for young people."     - Andrea Davis Pinkney, Executive Director, Scholastic

"Reading for meaning opens opportunities for a lifetime of learning. Providing emerging readers with engaging texts that are designed to offer both challenges and support for each individual will improve their lives for years to come. Storyshares is a wonderful start."
- David Rose, Co-founder of CAST & UDL

# The Whipping Words

Megan Dean

STORYSHARES

Story Share, Inc.
New York. Boston. Philadelphia

Storyshares
Story Share, Inc.
24 N. Bryn Mawr Avenue #340
Bryn Mawr, PA 19010-3304
www.storyshares.org

*Inspiring reading with a new kind of book.*

**Interest Level:** Middle School
**Grade Level Equivalent:** 4.0

9781642612110

Book design by Storyshares

Printed in the United States of America

Storyshares Presents

# 1

I lifted my eyes from my newest book. Its mesmerizing smell was enough to keep me from putting it down. A small boy in the corner of my classroom raised his grimy little hand and flung it around like a snake, flailing to and fro. I nodded at him in acknowledgement, and he set his hand back down on his desk full of classwork I gave him.

"Miss May, when'll we learn to read like you?" he stammered, as his cheeks flushed a red darker than Julia Gates' prize-winning apples.

I tucked a blonde curl of mine behind my ear, a nervous habit I had that my mama used to rap my knuckles for when I was young. Before I could respond, a sudden flood of old memories gushed into my head.

It started with one from when I was just a baby. It wasn't vivid, nor did the memory have movement. It was solely an image, an image of a black woman's arms swaddling my small white body. Tula was her name, at least the only name I knew her by. Never did it phase me that I had a white mama and a white papa but a Black nanny. To me, she was a friend and a good one at that.

My mind flashed next to my seventh birthday, when Mama and Papa bought me a new doll. I named her Little Tula and was instantly scorned for wanting my beautiful doll to be associated with a Negro. At the time, my little mind was blind to the racism so heavily practiced by my parents, neighbors, and peers.

Tula was my friend and more of a mother than the pasty, worrisome one that I had been given. My pa was never seen much. He was often off checking in with the slave-holder, Tom, or talking cotton with the husbands of mama's friends. Tula's stories of her daddy became my definition of a daddy. We had an inseparable bond, or so I thought.

Along with turning seven came a tutor for my reading skills. Her name was Ms. Turpil-Rey. She was snarky, cruel, and my worst nightmare. I often left her sessions crying, bruised, and hating reading more than I had before. She also said she hated my curls once, and that was enough to set off a life-long insecurity.

Still, I had my Tula. Her warm, large body was always waiting for me by the window seat of my nursery because she wasn't allowed near the tutor. To be frank, I wouldn't have wanted that tutor near her. Tula would smile at me, stand, wipe her hands down on her apron, and place a secretive kiss on my brow.

Every day she'd ask, "D'you learn anyfang, angel?"

My responses were typically a "yess'm," or a "only that I hate readin'" or a "no'm, I wasn't listening."

She would smile and hand me my doll, and we'd begin playing.

One day, our usual routine was broken as I finished my lesson, and she was nowhere in the room.

# 2

"Tula, Tula, are you hidin'?" I chuckled and pounced on my bouncy bed, thinking she was causing the lumps. No nanny. I bounded to the closet and slammed the doors open. No nanny.

I turned to go fetch my mama and clasped down on the handle of my door. When I creaked the door open, a certain buzz echoed from the parlor. I ran down the staircase, my blue fluffed dress swooshing at the same time as my footsteps pounded the wooden stairs. The buzz turned into a small, quiet hum.

"Mama?"

The hum turned silent, and my mother's heels clicked my way. She put on a fake smile and rushed me back to the nursery. Her group of friends stood at the base of the staircase and through gritted teeth she snarled, "You ruined my party, May. Go play with that fool, Tula. You'll learn the importance of one of your mama's gatherings one of these days."

I sighed and sat down on the window seat as my mama closed my door sharply. I stroked the spine of the new book Ms. Turpil-Rey and I were working on. I'd read it three times already. Of course, she wouldn't have known that because I pretended like I didn't know the first words.

My gaze zoomed out to the plantation. It looked empty in the fields. Tufts of white cotton were mere specks from my window. Not a single slave was in the fields. My eyes darted then to the right, where about a dozen slave houses were nestled neatly and compactly. A crowd of black bodies was gathered there.

I sat up a little straighter because I knew they weren't supposed to be over there. I popped my window open a bit, praying I could hear something, but it was only a buzz, like my mother's party. Two acres was too far to eavesdrop.

I pushed my window all of the way open. The circle was just large enough for me to sneak through. A white, chipped-paint terrace stretched down to the base of the back lawn. I slipped off my shiny, black, strap-on shoes and left them neat on the seat as I flung my legs out of the window. The two seconds of my toes searching for the terrace were terrifying, but once I got my footing, I was ready to climb down.

One scraped knee and two torn stockings later, I was safely on the ground and sprinting through the back gate on the lawn. The rocky path that led to the fields sloped down a steep hill. I tended to bound down it, but this time I'd have to go down slowly and quietly.

As I got closer, the slave houses got nearer, and the buzz evolved into screams and yells. I snuck behind one of the houses and attempted to see what everyone was yelling about.

My eyes were not anticipating what I would come to find. A young man, perhaps sixteen, collapsed in the middle of a crowd. A better-dressed Negro, presumably the slaveholder, was beating him mercilessly. His arms came down with such force that the whip he was using to inflict pain hardly had enough time to curve and snap. A large man shuffled and blocked my view.

"Stoppit, Tom, please!" many slaves screamed. A woman in the back of the crowd crumpled to her knees as the boy gave a blood curdling cry and gasped for his last breath. The rhythmic smacking of the whip stopped, and the crowd scattered, some moving quicker than others. The woman looked up from her tear-covered hands, slowly rose, and walked towards the motionless boy's body.

She glanced around, ensuring Tom was nowhere nearby and placed a tender kiss on his bloody brow. Then she turned in my direction, and I instinctively sprinted back up the hill, into the house, and up to my room. I sat on my bed, pondering what I had just seen.

# 3

About an hour later, Tula slowly entered my room. I crossed my legs, hoping she wouldn't see the tears in my stockings.

Her eyes were puffy and her cheeks red. "Hiya baby," she choked, and slumped onto the window seat. She flattened her apron as she sat. "I know you watched that, May. You shouldn't have been there."

"Neither should you've Tula!" I stammered. "Who was he? What happened? Does Mama know?"

"Hush! 'Nough questions," she hissed, as a slow tear streaked down her face.

"You know him?" I asked after awhile of silence.

"Yes'm. He was my baby. My last one. He was a gentle soul, wouldn't hurt a fly," she paused, choking on her words. "Tom caught him pocketing some cotton . . . he liked to look at plants."

My heart dropped to my stomach. "Can't my mama or papa help?"

Her brow sharpened, and she stood. Her finger pointed straight at me. "Look atcho skin, May! Look at it! You're white as your porcelain doll. I'm black as the darkest night. Your color ain't never gonna help me out. Ain't never gonna help any of us out!"

"No, no . . . I can help!"

"No, no," she laughed, "you can't. You know what we want? We want what you have. We want even the things you hate, child."

"No one would want to read," I grumbled.

"My baby boy wanted to. want to. Every one of 'em Negroes hauling your cotton wants to. We get nothing but whips and heartache, baby," she snapped and sat back down, covering her face in her hands.

I reached behind my pillow where I hid the newest book Ms. Turpil-Rey gave me. I pulled it out and traced the intricate gold patterns that surrounded the title. "It's 'bout a princess who isn't happy being locked up in a tower. She's so beautiful, but the wicked people won't let her go. Tula, ain't that cruel?" I explained as Tula uncovered her face.

"Yes baby. I know it is." Seriousness flashed over her sullen face. "What happens to her?"

"I dunno, haven't read that far. I hope she gets freed so she can be like the other princesses." I flipped to the last pages, skimming the sea of words quickly.

"Child, don't do that! That'll spoil it, won't it?"

"Yes'm."

"Just read it . . . don't spoil it. You wanna know what happens to her?"

I nodded.

"Then find out. Your wants may be tricky to get . . ." she paused, "but the fight will pay off, child. Dear Lord, let it pay off!" She teared up and quickly prepared me for bed, tucked me in, said a prayer, and slipped out my door.

At the time, I remember thinking Tula really was foolish for crying out to God over the ending of a book. I didn't realize until I was much older that just possibly she was crying for something more.

The next morning, Tula was sitting on the window seat extra early. I sat up in bed and flattened my frizzy hair.

"What are you . . ." I started.

"I couldn't sleep. May, can you read your story to me?" she said hurriedly.

"I guess so." I shuffled in my comforter until my feet found the cold floor. I rubbed my sleepy eyes and grabbed the book from my nightstand. I flipped to the first page. "I'll just start over for ya, Tula."

A smile cracked on her still-sullen face as I did my best to make my reading exciting. My voice would crescendo, and she'd lean in, elbows on her knees and head in her palms. Her face would change with the story, and I finally realized why reading could be a blessing: emotion.

My stomach grumbled, and I closed the book. Tula snapped back into reality and quickly sent me down the stairs to have breakfast. My mother was at the table sipping coffee and rolling her nails on the wood surface, showing her irritation. My father was heading out to town and planted a kiss on both my mother's and my face on his way out the door. Mama and I ate in silence. When the meal was through, I quickly went back to my room. I caught Tula thumbing the pages of the book, and in embarrassment, she set it back down.

"Tula, I could teach you how to read it," I smiled.

Her face lit up but quickly darkened again. "No baby, I'm not allowed to. It's against the law."

"But it'd be a secret! I won't tell."

* * *

She refused my proposal many times, but her curiosity increased daily. She wondered how to spell a name or what letter was which. By the end of one month,

I had read eight books to her. On the ninth book, she finally asked to read a page.

"Try it, Tula. You can do it."

She stuttered a word at a time, letter by letter, sound by sound. Her sentences were rigid and choppy, but she managed. Her words became smoother as time progressed, and my seven-year-old pride grew.

*I'm teaching a slave to read*, I thought. *I'm teaching a friend to read*.

Another month passed, but this time it was Tula who read five books. Our little secret was successfully creating a lifelong love for literature for the both of us.

# 4

One night after Ms. Turpil-Rey's lecture was over and Tula had tucked me into bed and left, my mama came in. I was surprised at first because she normally avoided my nighttime routine. She sat down at the foot of the bed.

"Ms. Turpil-Rey says you've done so much better in reading as of late. She's told me you don't need her help anymore," she said. Then she whispered words I never heard her say before. "I'm proud of you."

There was an eerily long moment of silence that I finally broke. "What'll I do now that I don't have lessons?"

"Tomorrow you're sitting in on one of my parties! Isn't that exciting?"

I wanted to groan. That meant getting fancy and acting fancy too.

"I even bought you a new dress! I'll go fetch it real quick." Mama left my room, and it was in that moment of her getting the gift that I realized how conditional her love was. She only loved me when I was going her way. She invested in me what she thought important. Never what I thought important. She returned with a charming dress made of vibrant sunflower fabric, and after I tried it on, she left and bid me goodnight.

# 5

It was midnight, yes, midnight . . . I remember the grandfather clock donging twelve times, when something else strange happened. My door creaked open, and a little silhouette tip-toed into my room. My feet shook with fear, and my lip trembled as I peeped open one eye and watched the figure rummage through my books. I figured it was a monster, a terrible beast out for my blood.

Actually, it was a young boy . . . I could tell when his black face met the moon's light shooting from the window. There was a slave child in my room.

I wanted to yell, but his facial expressions seemed urgent as he'd hold a book to the window light and place it back down. He did this until he found the one he was apparently looking for. He ran out of my room so quickly that his silhouette seemed to have disappeared on the spot. I jumped to my window seat and looked out to see him and many other slaves gathered outside the fence like a pack of wolves. I watched them for awhile, fighting a diligent battle against my heavy eyelids.

I couldn't help it. I snuck out of the house and followed the book thief and the others. The wet grass tickled my feet until I went past the gate, where, instead, I was greeted by abrasive gravel. The chill of the night's air numbed my cheeks and hands as I chased down the little boy. He was fast, but my curiosity was faster. I spied him as they all entered a slave house on the edge of the property line. The door's hinges creaked with each new entrance.

The slaves flooded in for what seemed like forever, and those who couldn't fit inside peeked in the small windows until those too held all the eyes they could. I had had it! That dumb child took the book I was reading with Tula and my fury led me to march through the sea of slaves. They murmured quietly as I walked through the house to the center of the room.

I stuck out my arm towards the little thief. "I'll have my book."

He hesitated putting it in my hand but finally did.

I began to walk out.

"Miss, you ain't gon' tell, is ya?" his voice quivered.

"Course I ain't gon' tell! It's a good book." Every slave there seemed to hold on to each of my words. "I'd've stole it too." I said no more and left the house.

# 6

The next day started early as Mama, not Tula, woke me up and dressed me. She tied back my spring-tight curls gently in a black ribbon. We quickly ate breakfast and then waited patiently in the parlor for her guests to arrive. The waiting game was agonizing, but my mother seemed to not be able to contain herself. She ran through manners and how to greet her friends and how to sit at least seven times before her friends began arriving.

We greeted them and thus began the most boring two and a half hours of my life. We started with tea, or should I say, I drank tea while the ladies drank up each other's gossip.

"I heard, Cynthia, that Penelope Smith, she . . ." and gasps.

"Well, I heard Samantha did . . ." and gasps. They were so caught up in the gossip that I luckily had to do no talking the whole time. When Mama's last guest left, she plopped onto the fainting sofa and sat there with a wild grin.

"D'you have fun?" she asked. I was taken aback for a moment, as it was the first time I'd heard her slur her words. I nodded. "Well good. This is what being a big girl is all about! Being hospitable, understanding your town . . ." She continued justifying her gossip while walking me back to the nursery. We embraced at the top of the stairs, and for that meager moment, all was well.

Mama opened the door, and before I could put one shiny, black shoe in the room, she screamed. "What are you doing? What are you doing?" Mama turned to me. "May, get your papa!" Without thinking, I sprinted down the stairs and through the back gate, down to the field where my father was intensely observing the slaves.

"Papa, papa! Something's wrong. I was . . . then mama . . . oh papa, hurry!" I panted, heart pounding and blood rushing. We jogged together back up the hill and into the house. The slaveholder came with us, and suddenly my stomach lurched. Tula was in trouble.

I pushed past the people crowding my door and crouched down by Tula, who had a bruise spreading across her face. I held her hand but was quickly pulled away by an observing male slave.

"We don't wantchu hurt, miss May. You did this for us," he whispered into my ear.

Tom interjected, "What's going on here?"

The story they wanted him to hear unfolded. Tula had forced little May to teach her how to read. She deliberately broke the slave code for the past few months. Not only this, she had taught most, if not all the other slaves to read as well. She claimed it to be for joy, but the true reason was to empower the slaves to feel equal. Every night, she'd send a little boy to collect a book from the pile in little May's room, so a lesson on reading could quietly take place in her house.

I felt stabbed by every untruthful word coming out of their mouths. "It's not true," I choked, but little sound came out. "It's not true."

# 7

Our secret was dead, and it seemed as if the slaves' joy was too.

The next day was eerily quiet until noon. Every slave suspected of learning to read was whipped. Young screams. Old screams. Women's screams. Men's screams. They echoed off the property like a demonic chorus. My mother, father, and I watched as Tom lay his wrath on each one of them. Tula reared the line. Tom's jawline tightened and so did my clenched fists.

"Anything to say, teacher?" Tom mocked. Silently, Tula got to her knees and prepared for the whip to meet her back.

Smack.

She said nothing.

Did nothing.

Tom lashed out harder and harder. The whip got louder and louder, but Tula said nothing.

When he was done, she stood, took a few steps, then yelled in her deepest, most booming voice, "You may whip us. You may get right in our face. You may strap us in chains, but we can be free! The whipping words we read didn't change our status, but they changed our freedom! We freed our minds!"

With a final crack of the whip, there was silence, the most agonizing sound of all. A day passed and still, silence. A month passed . . . a year, and silence remained.

Tula was gone. I never saw her again, but her spirit resided in me every time I flipped open a book.

* * *

"Miss May? Miss May?" the little boy asked me again. "When will we learn to read like you?"

I swallowed my emotions. "As soon as you decide to free your mind."

# About The Author

Megan Dean has had the dream of becoming an author since the second grade and couldn't be more overjoyed to finally share her words with the world. Megan's interest in writing is the result of an active imagination, a love for words, and seeing the world through different lenses.

Dedication to her passions is a staple in her life, whether it be working vigorously in her academics, racing her heart out on the track or cross country course, or persuing her faith. Writing, however, has been at the backbone of it all, giving her a way to express herself as she sees the world and to string together stories of the lives of her characters.

Over the years, she has developed a love for historical fiction, yet looks forward to broadening her horizons and having fun with other genres. Of course, Megan would not be where she is now had it not been for the series of doors the Lord has opened for her, the constant motivation from teachers and coaches, and the support of friends and family.

# About The Publisher

Story Shares is a nonprofit focused on supporting the millions of teens and adults who struggle with reading by creating a new shelf in the library specifically for them. The ever-growing collection features content that is compelling and culturally relevant for teens and adults, yet still readable at a range of lower reading levels.

Story Shares generates content by engaging deeply with writers, bringing together a community to create this new kind of book. With more intriguing and approachable stories to choose from, the teens and adults who have fallen behind are improving their skills and beginning to d scover the joy of reading. For more information, vis t storyshares.org.

Easy to Read. Hard to Pu: Down.

# The Whipping Words

www.ingramcontent.com/pod-product-compliance
Lightning Source LLC
Chambersburg PA
CBHW071229170626
46809CB00005BA/1997